Augustus

Duncan

dylia

Isaiah Maria

kirsten

Julia M.

SAPAY

San

Nick Anna

gerundich

Caitlin

Liana Emma

Sparkle

Elios

Carlos

Lilan

Emma

E

Jock

Sl.

i

Dana!!

i

Asher

Sandra

a

Maya

Jamie

m

Cherry

Charlotte

Sophie E.

Blake

come
and
play

Children of Our World Having Fun

Poems by children

Edited by **Ayana Lowe**

Pictures from Magnum Photos

To my students, who always "tell on themselves."
And to the wisest kid I know, Mom.

Excerpt from Rita Dove © 1995 by World Poetry, Inc.
From an interview with Grace Cavalieri published by *The American Poetry Review*

Map courtesy of Cartographic Research Lab, University of Alabama

Published by Bloomsbury U.S.A. Children's Books
175 Fifth Avenue, New York, New York 10010
Distributed to the trade by Macmillan

Library of Congress Cataloging-in-Publication Data
Come and play : children of our world having fun / poems by children ; edited by Ayana Lowe ;
photographs from the Magnum Collection.
p.   cm.
ISBN-13: 978-1-59990-245-6 · ISBN-10: 1-59990-245-1 (hardcover)
ISBN-13: 978-1-59990-246-3 · ISBN-10: 1-59990-246-X (reinforced)
1. Children's poetry. 2. Children—Portraits. I. Lowe, Ayana.
PN6109.97.C648 2008   808.81'0083—dc22   2007039970

Book design by Daniel Roode
Typeset in ChaletPS

First U.S. Edition 2008
Printed in China
(hardcover) 10 9 8 7 6 5 4 3 2 1
(reinforced) 10 9 8 7 6 5 4 3 2 1

All papers used by Bloomsbury U.S.A. are natural, recyclable products
made from wood grown in well-managed forests. The manufacturing processes
conform to the environmental regulations of the country of origin.

I think all of us have moments, particularly in our childhood, where we come alive, maybe for the first time. And we go back to those moments and think, "This is when I became myself."

—Rita Dove,
Poet Laureate of the United States,
1993–1995

Merry-Go-Round

Fun feels like happy.

Swinging feels like

dangling from the ceiling.

Laughing feels like

jumping on the bed.

Go as far as you can.

And if you can't do it anymore . . .

stop!

West Belfast, Northern Ireland, 1978

Sophia's Schemes

They don't know we are here.

I like to play pranks.

I like to be very sly.

Follow me.

Near Agadir, Morocco, 2000

Fun Is a Motion

Fun is a motion.

Something that you really like.

Trying to fly, you feel a tingling
sensation inside of you.

Yippee!

Village of Horcones, Chile, 1957

The Proving Ground

Ping.

Pong.

The sound the ball makes.

Holding the paddle like that.

They know what they are doing.

The champions of recess.

Couldn't Help It

Bubble bath.

Giggle, laugh.

Oops.

She just fell in.

That's what she's laughing about.

The problem is it's over too quickly.

It's getting dark out.

One more time.

North Yorkshire, England, 2005

Papa!

I want to kiss the water.

Let me go.

Golfe-Juan, France, 1951

Looking Out

The camera catches their eyes
through the window.
Don't they look like
they are playing on a school bus?
That girl in the middle
is looking at something else.
She is not interested
in the camera.

Vientiane, Laos, 1994

Jazz

Concentrating.

I'm thinking what move I should

do next.

I am having fun.

A Waterfall

Two people.

Different places.

Rocks rough and smooth.

Water fast and slow.

One calm.

One excited.

Wait, I'm coming up!

Wait, I'm coming down!

Ein Gedi, Israel, 1967

Mom would say.

Massa Marittima, Italy, 2004

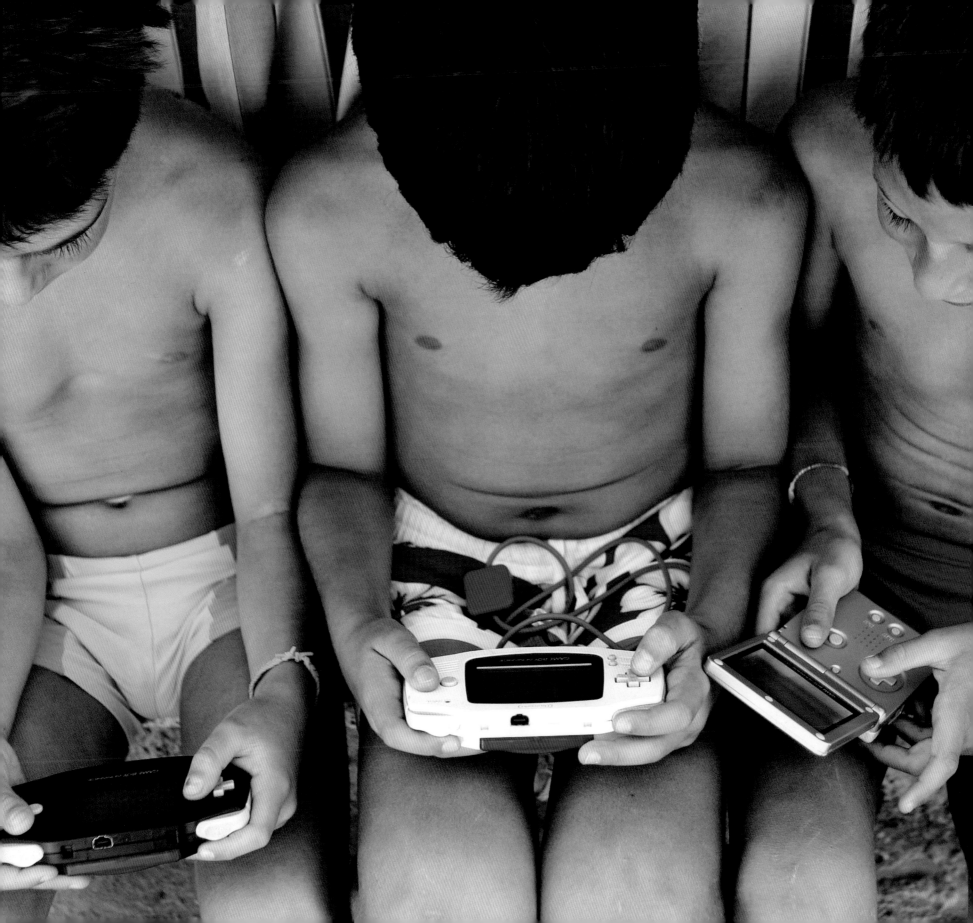

Why?

Maybe she's scared.

Donegal County, Ireland, 1995

Shhh, I'm Thinking

Up in the sky.

Will it fly?

Maybe if it catches

a good gust of wind.

How do all the parts work?

Could I make something like that?

Masqat, Oman, 1975

A Tight Squeeze

Wet and happy.

The beach is hot.

I've saved you a spot.

Wonsan City, North Korea, 1982

Performing near waves
is good for your rhythm.
Go! Go!
Shimmy! Shimmy!
It's fun to make jokes and plans
with friends after the dance.

Abidjan, Ivory Coast, 1972

In the night
our ice sculpture comes alive
but we are too cold to move a lot.
We get warmth from petting our
magical dog.
Have you ever seen the aurora?

Alta, Norway, 2001

It's Easy

The gymnast
standing on one hand.
Looking at the sand.
Maybe she sees a crab?

Cornwall, England, 1989

Walking on air.

Looks ancient.

Mmm.

I'd like to do this.

I like adventure.

Hard work.

I'd tell him to keep going.

Village of Karamakhi, Republic of Dagestan, 2000

Tag

In tag, you improve your running.

You improve your escape time.

When you are playing tag,

you are in a whole other world.

Nothing else could be better.

Baghdad, Iraq, 2003

On a Boat

My hat!

No! It's my hat.

No! My hat.

Don't take my hat.

No! No! No!

Bangkok, Thailand, 1999

Surprise!

Playtime.

Playtime.

What is he doing?

What is his name?

Lampasas, Texas, USA, 1990

You trip someone by pulling their feet.

It's called low offense.

Go, go, go!

You can get him.

France, 1995

The Humanoids

Stay in your row.

Stay in your seat.

Do not wiggle or move your feet.

LIFT OFF!

It's not a Disney ride.

But what happens
when you look inside?

Rosy Cheeks

I am the teddy bear.

Cozy.

In the back.

If you make the picture bigger,

maybe you'll be able to see

the snow dogs pulling.

The dogs wear socks

to keep their feet warm.

Alta, Norway, 2001

String Tales

Looking at Grandpa's hands.

Different string shapes.

Cat's whiskers.

Good job.

You are learning.

Anaktuvuk, Alaska, 1953

Marshmallows

Come back here!

This instant!

Swimming away.

Paddle, paddle.

In marshmallow boats.

Tawitawi, Philippines, 1995

Brixton Road

Skipping.

Outside, afterschoolish.

Homework?

Or a list to go to the store?

She feels famous.

South London, England, 1964

1
Ferdinando Scianna (Italian)
1999
Sanaa, Yemen

2
Henri Cartier-Bresson (French)
1959
A carnival ride in Lorraine, France

3
Chris Steele-Perkins (British)
1978
Outside Divis Flats, an apartment block in
West Belfast, Northern Ireland

4
Gueorgui Pinkhassov (French/Russian)
2000
The grocery store in a small village built
around the lighthouse of the Cap Ghir, near the
town of Agadir, Morocco

5
Sergio Larrain (Chilean)
1957
Daughters of fishermen in the village
of Horcones, Chile

6
Bruno Barbey (Moroccan-born/French)
1980
Playing Ping-Pong on a homemade table in the
workers' district of Tchao Yang in Shanghai, China

7
Harry Gruyaert (Belgian)
1995
Marrakech, Morocco

8
Peter Marlow (British)
2005
Sledding at Christmas in Richmond,
North Yorkshire, England

9
Robert Capa (Hungarian)
1951
Pablo Picasso and his young son, Claude,
in Golfe-Juan, France

10
Abbas (Iranian)
1994
Vientiane, Laos

11
Guy Le Querrec (French)
2001
American jazz musician Wynton Marsalis playing chess
with a local boy at a jazz festival in Marciac, in the
Midi-Pyrénées region of France. Mr. Marsalis sent him a
trumpet from New York to encourage him to play

12
Leonard Freed (American)
1967
Waterfalls of Ein Gedi, in the Dead Sea region of Israel

13
Ferdinando Scianna (Italian)
2004
On a beach in Massa Marittima, Italy

14
Martine Franck (Belgian)
1995
Tory Island, Donegal County, Ireland

15
René Burri (Swiss)
1975
Playing with a wooden airplane in Masqat, Oman

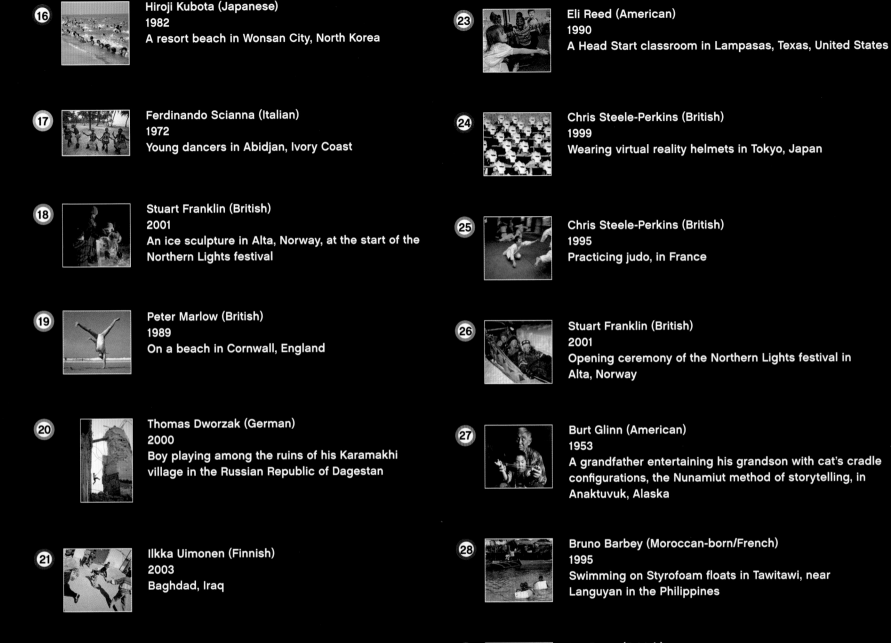

16
Hiroji Kubota (Japanese)
1982
A resort beach in Wonsan City, North Korea

17
Ferdinando Scianna (Italian)
1972
Young dancers in Abidjan, Ivory Coast

18
Stuart Franklin (British)
2001
An ice sculpture in Alta, Norway, at the start of the
Northern Lights festival

19
Peter Marlow (British)
1989
On a beach in Cornwall, England

20
Thomas Dworzak (German)
2000
Boy playing among the ruins of his Karamakhi
village in the Russian Republic of Dagestan

21
Ilkka Uimonen (Finnish)
2003
Baghdad, Iraq

22
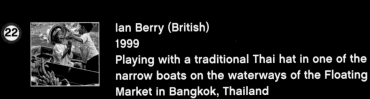
Ian Berry (British)
1999
Playing with a traditional Thai hat in one of the
narrow boats on the waterways of the Floating
Market in Bangkok, Thailand

23
Eli Reed (American)
1990
A Head Start classroom in Lampasas, Texas, United States

24
Chris Steele-Perkins (British)
1999
Wearing virtual reality helmets in Tokyo, Japan

25
Chris Steele-Perkins (British)
1995
Practicing judo, in France

26
Stuart Franklin (British)
2001
Opening ceremony of the Northern Lights festival in
Alta, Norway

27
Burt Glinn (American)
1953
A grandfather entertaining his grandson with cat's cradle
configurations, the Nunamiut method of storytelling, in
Anaktuvuk, Alaska

28

Bruno Barbey (Moroccan-born/French)
1995
Swimming on Styrofoam floats in Tawitawi, near
Languyan in the Philippines

29
Ian Berry (British)
1964
Skipping down a Brixton street in
South London, England

Where on earth were the photographs taken?

To find the location where each photograph was taken, you can match the numbers on this map to the numbers on the previous two pages.

North
America

South
America

About the Writers

More than 140 children from New York City contributed their "word riffs" and poetry to *Come and Play*. Many attended Hunter College Elementary School during the 2006–07 school year, while others, such as the children shown here (photo taken by Idris Purnell), attended Hunter's 2007 summer school classes. Ayana Lowe is the fifth person from the right in the bottom row. The children included Sasha Domnitz's first-grade class, Inna Kofman's first-grade class, Gilda Sall's second-grade class, Marie Rhone's second-grade class, Heather Wagner's third-grade class, Michele Boyum's fourth-grade class, Denise Rohan-Jones's fourth-grade class, Natalie Berthold's fifth-grade class, and Molly Michalec's fifth-grade class.

A heartfelt thanks to all of the children who generously contributed their hearts and words to this project. A special thanks to those who worked extra hard as our time began running out: Jamie Crook, Isaiah Milbauer, Charlotte Milbauer, Jeremiah Milbauer, Gus Pearl, and Henry Pearl.

About the Photographers

This photograph was taken at Magnum's 1988 annual meeting at Fenelon College in Paris by photographer Elliott Erwitt. The photographers who can be identified include Thomas Hoepker, Eve Arnold, George Rodger, Ian Berry, Erich Hartmann, Abbas, Philip Jones Griffiths, Bruno Barbey, Josef Koudelka, Martine Franck, and Susan Meiselas. Magnum now has forty-nine members throughout the world.

Should I Tell On Myself?

One day in early September, as the last two giggling first graders scurried from my class for recess, I overheard one curly-headed fellow call to his pal, a lanky little guy with twinkling dark eyes: "Should I tell on myself?" Before I could hear his friend's reply, they were out of sight, racing toward the playground. Had he done something naughty? Immediately I thought about this funny question, "Should I tell on myself?" I smiled. "Yes, tell on yourself!" I thought. "Tell the world who you are."

As I headed toward the playground for lunch patrol, I saw the same little fellow roughing it with a rowdy group of children. They were laughing, tussling, running, pulling, shouting, hopping, jumping, and throwing. I observed how they began to fashion the rules for their play. They started by making a pecking order. One child became the immediate leader; she was the one who gave orders. The leader chose the second in command and this child chose her sidekicks—the two pals from my class. Under the watchful eyes of the leader, the two boys chose a few others. I immediately felt a deep empathy for those who weren't picked.

Children "tell on themselves" when they play. Every emotion is experienced: hurt, anger, embarrassment, envy, joy, ecstasy, fascination, loneliness, and sorrow. In play, a child can safely experience what in the larger world may turn dangerous. Play's safety gives children the freedom and support to tell the world who they are.

When recess was over, the magic ended and the flurry of activity halted as quickly as it had begun. "Time's up, line up," the principal yelled. As I opened the front door of the school to let the children in, I listened to the chatter. Observing their whispers, gestures, and facial expressions, I was privy to the children's secrets. I could hear them talking about what had happened during recess. I learned that someone got hurt, someone felt powerful, someone was left out, and two children even became blood brothers. For those forty minutes, every child "told on themselves"—expressing to their classmates who they were. And when the next day came, those children wanted to do it all over again.

Ayana Lowe

CHARLOTTE

Danielle

Aidan

Sophie

Rosa

Thomas

Alex

Amelia

Ayanna

Joey